Guido van Genechten
Max and the Moon
First published in Belgium by Clavis Uitgeverij
Amsterdam-Hasselt 2007.
Text and illustrations © Clavis Uitgeverij
Amsterdam-Hasselt, 2007. All rights reserved.

First published in the UK by the National Maritime Museum,
Greenwich, London, SE10 9NF in 2007.
www.nmm.ac.uk/publishing
978-0-948065-85-9

GUIDO VAN GENECHTEN

Max and the Moon

NATIONAL MARITIME MUSEUM

ROYAL OBSERVATORY GREENWICH

Max loves playing in the sunshine all day.
The sun's warm beams give life to everything
and make things grow.

But the sun gets tired shining all day.
In the evening the sun sinks away.
Shadows grow and darkness falls.
The sun goes to sleep.
It is nearly bedtime for Max too.

Max gets ready for bed.
He puts on his pyjamas all by himself.
He turns on his bedside light
and takes his elephant from the windowsill.

Suddenly, a thousand million lights switch on outside.
The lights are stars.
They are waiting for the moon to rise, just like Max.

Oh, there is the moon!
'Hello, moon,' Max whispers.
'Nice to see you again.
Will you stay with me all night?'

'Yes ...' the moon smiles.
'Turn off your bedside light and close your eyes.
I will shine for you all night.'

Max sleeps soundly, all night long,
while the moon shines high in the sky.
The moon watches over Max (and everyone else).
But of course the moon gets tired too...

In the morning the sun is shining again.
Max wakes up and has a big stretch.
'Hello, sun,' he says happily.
'I have had a good night's sleep.
Have you?'